KU-350-539

NATIONAL PARKS

By Sharon Fear

Series Literacy Consultant
Dr Ros Fisher

Pearson Education Limited
Edinburgh Gate
Harlow
Essex CM20 2JE
England

www.longman.co.uk

The right of Sharon Fear to be identified as the author of this Work has been asserted by her in accordance with the Copyright, Designs and Patents Act, 1988.

Text Copyright © 2004 Pearson Education Limited. Compilation Copyright © 2004 Dorling Kindersley Ltd. All rights reserved. No part of this publication may be reproduced, stored in a retrieval system or transmitted in any form or by any means electronic, mechanical, photocopying, recording, or otherwise, without either the prior written permission of the publishers and copyright owners or a licence permitting restricted copying in the United Kingdom issued by the Copyright Licensing Agency Ltd., 90 Tottenham Court Road, London W1P 9HE

ISBN 0 582 84539 4

Colour reproduction by Colourscan, Singapore
Printed and bound in China by Leo Paper Products Ltd.

The Publisher's policy is to use paper manufactured from sustainable forests.

The following people from **DK** have
contributed to the development of this product:

Art Director Rachael Foster

Ross George, Carole Oliver **Design**	**Managing Editor** Scarlett O'Hara
Helen McFarland **Picture Research**	**Editorial** Kate Pearce, Amanda Rayner
Ed Merritt **Cartography**	**Production** Rosalind Holmes
Richard Czapnik, Andy Smith **Cover Design**	**DTP** David McDonald

Consultant David Green

Dorling Kindersley would like to thank: Ann Cannings and Clive Savage for design assistance, Johnny Pau for additional cover design work.

Picture Credits: Corbis: 24tl, 30b; W. Perry Conway 16tl; Pat O'Hara 7tr; Galen Rowell 13b; Patrick Ward 17b. Gerald Cubitt: 27cl. Eye Ubiquitous: Derek Cattani 29b. FLPA – Images of nature: Tom and Pam Gardner 5br; Tony Hamblin 15tr; Minden Pictures 26–27; Mark Newman 12tl; Silvestris 10bc; Larry West 30tr. Getty Images: Gavin Hellier 9br. Robert Harding Picture Library: Geoff Renner 10–11. Lonely Planet Images: Trevor Creighton 25br. National Geographic Image Collection: Bill Hatcher 8br. Nature Picture Library: Ingo Arndt 5cr; Nigel Bean 1; John Cancalosi 8tl; David Curl 24cl; Jeff Foott 4br; William Osborn 25tr; Anup Shah 28b; Jeremy Walker 6–7. N.H.P.A: 18–19, 19tr, 21tr, 21b; Andy Rouse 28cr. Pictures Colour Library: Picture Finders 13tr. Woodfall Wild Images: 14–15. Jacket: ImageState/Pictor: front t. Vireo: W. Peckover front bl.

All other images: ⬚ Dorling Kindersley © 2004. For further information see www.dkimages.com
Dorling Kindersley Ltd., 80 Strand, London WC2R ORL

Contents

What Are National Parks?

The world is home to millions of **species** of plants and animals. National parks all over the world help preserve many wonderful landforms, plants and animals.

A national park is an area of land that is protected by a nation's government. Most protect animals, plants and natural landscapes. Some parks protect historic places. A few protect the **culture**, or way of life, of the **native people** who live in them. Mining, farming, building and hunting are usually banned in national parks. The aim is to keep the land untouched and the plants and animals safe from humans.

Grand Canyon National Park, United States

Kruger National Park, South Africa

Creation of National Parks

In 1872 the world's first national park was opened. This was Yellowstone National Park in the US. Yellowstone has 10,000 hot springs and 200 **geysers** like this one. Today there are more than 4,000 national parks around the world.

◾ Glacier National Park, Canada

◾ Lake District National Park, England

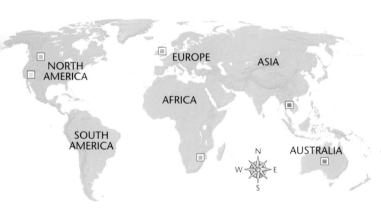

◾ Khao Yai National Park, Thailand

The national parks in this book are from different regions of the world. Each has been set up for a different reason. This book looks at six national parks and explains how each one is unique. However, all these parks have two common goals. One is to protect the park and the other is to teach people about the natural wonders found there.

◾ Uluru-Kata Tjuta National Park, Australia

Grand Canyon National Park, United States

The Grand Canyon National Park has 2 billion years of the Earth's history carved in rock. It is found in Arizona in the United States. The park spans almost 5 thousand square kilometres and has about 5 million visitors each year.

The Grand Canyon was set up as a national park in 1919 for several reasons: first to protect the **native people**, second to protect the wildlife and third to protect the landscape.

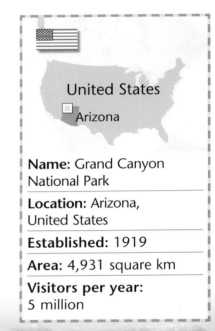

United States

Arizona

Name: Grand Canyon National Park

Location: Arizona, United States

Established: 1919

Area: 4,931 square km

Visitors per year: 5 million

The Landscape

The Grand Canyon is one of the world's deepest **canyons**. It measures nearly 2 kilometres down at its deepest point and about 29 kilometres across at its widest point. The canyon is 445 kilometres long.

About 40 layers of rock make the canyon walls. These layers have built up over 2 billion years. At the bottom of the canyon the rock is so old that it existed long before dinosaurs lived on the Earth.

How the Canyon Formed

The canyon is a **plateau** that was slowly raised up. Then wind and rain gradually wore it down. Later the Colorado River carved out the canyon. It carried away tonnes of rock every year. Today the river is still carving into the canyon.

Mexican spotted owl

Wildlife

The Grand Canyon has several **habitats** and hundreds of different animals live in different parts of the Grand Canyon. Many of these animal **species** are rare and **endangered**.

Near the river, coyotes, skunks, tree frogs and rattlesnakes are found. Above the inner canyon, thousands of bats and many California Condors fly in the sky.

In the forests, lizards and owls make their homes. More than fifty different types of mammals live there, too. These include porcupines, black bears, foxes and elk.

grey fox

porcupine

People and the Park

Native Americans have lived in the park for thousands of years. Today only about 600 Native Americans live in the remote inner canyon. There is a museum in the park that describes their history.

The Grand Canyon is in danger of **erosion** and pollution from so many visitors. So **park rangers** make sure that visitors take care of the park. This means it will be around for future generations to enjoy, too.

Some visitors ride mules to the bottom of the canyon.

The Havasu Falls is found in the inner canyon.

Glacier National Park, Canada

Glacier National Park is an icy wilderness full of snow-capped mountains rivers and waterfalls. It is found in British Columbia, Canada. The park spans about 1,349 square kilometres and has about 600 thousand visitors each year.

This area was set up as a national park in 1886 to protect the wildlife and the landscape. It now provides a safe home for many **endangered species**.

British Columbia

Canada

Name: Glacier National Park

Location: British Columbia, Canada

Established: 1886

Area: 1,349 square km

Visitors per year: 600,000

Avalanche

Avalanches crash down the mountains in the park. They are fast-moving flows of rock, snow and ice. Temperature changes or vibrations from loud noises or small earthquakes can cause an avalanche.

The Landscape

Glacier National Park is best known for its 400 **glaciers**. These slow-moving rivers of ice have helped carve out the park's rugged **terrain**.

There are many different climates and **habitats** in the park. High up in the mountains is the **alpine tundra**, where it is too cold for trees to grow. In the valleys is the **temperate rainforest**. It is one of the few cool and damp rainforests in the world.

Glaciers Change the Land

Glaciers form when snow falls in places where it's too cold to melt. As the snow builds up over many years, it turns to ice. When the build-up of ice becomes heavy, it begins to move slowly downhill, carrying rocks with it. These rocks grind against each other, causing **erosion**. Thousands of years ago this type of erosion created the park's deep valleys.

Cut-away of a Glacier

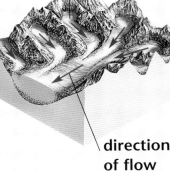

moving ice

direction of flow

Moose are strong swimmers and can cross large lakes.

Grizzly bears hibernate for half the year, so they look for enough food to last for six months.

Mountain goats climb the high mountain ledges.

Wildlife

Glacier National Park has many different animals. In the forests, deer, moose and elk wander around. In the valleys, black bears and grizzly bears search for berries. Along the rocky mountain ledges mountain goats look for plants.

Glacier National Park is an ideal home for the rare mountain caribou. They need lots of space to live, and wander freely throughout the whole park.

People and the Park

One of the biggest challenges for the **park rangers** is keeping visitors safe. Park rangers look out for signs of bad weather and possible avalanches.

The danger doesn't stop people coming to Glacier National Park. Visitors come to hike, climb, camp and ski. Park rangers also take care of the park and limit human activities to keep the landscape safe.

The Railway

The transcontinental railway links Canada from east to west and runs through the park. This makes the Glacier National Park very accessible to people. There is only one hotel for guests to stay in within the park. It was built at about the same time as the park was founded.

Rock climbing is a popular sport at Glacier National Park.

Lake District National Park, England

Lake District National Park is the largest of eight national parks in England. It is home to Scafell Pike – England's highest mountain. It is also home to Lake Windermere – England's largest lake.

The Lake District was set up as a national park in 1951. Unlike most national parks, about 42 thousand people live and work in the Lake District. They are, however, outnumbered by the sheep.

United Kingdom

England

Name: Lake District National Park

Location: North West England

Established: 1951

Area: 2,292 square km

Visitors per year: 12 million

The Landscape

Lake District National Park has one of the wildest landscapes in England. It is found in Cumbria, north west England. The park spans nearly 3 thousand square kilometres and has about 12 million visitors each year.

All the lakes were formed during the last ice age. As **glaciers** moved across the land, they carved out the lakes along the way. Then when the weather got warmer, the ice melted and filled the lakes with water.

Scafell Pike is England's highest mountain.

Lake Windermere is England's largest lake.

Wildlife

Lake District National Park has many different animals. Sheep, cows and horses graze in the valleys and pastures. In the mountain cliffs, peregrine falcons and osprey make their nests.

Beside the lakes, wading birds search for grubs while the natterjack toad hides. The vendace fish, an **endangered species**, swims along with the pike and trout in the lakes.

More peregrines live in the Lake District than anywhere else in Europe.

Otters live in the rivers within the park.

The natterjack toad blends into its surroundings.

People and the Park

People have lived in the Lake District for thousands of years. There have been important discoveries that show that Stone Age people hunted and farmed in this area. The Romans also built settlements and roads.

Visitors come to the park for lots of reasons. Some come to hike or watch birds. Others come to camp or swim. Students and scientists come to study the unique wildlife.

Kayaking is popular in the Lake District.

Walkers enjoy the landscape in the Lake District National Park.

Kruger National Park, South Africa

Kruger National Park is one of the largest parks in the world. It is found in the north east of South Africa. The park spans almost 20 thousand square kilometres and has about 500 thousand visitors each year.

This area was set up as a national park in 1898 to protect the wildlife and the landscape. It has saved the lives of many **endangered species**.

AFRICA

South Africa □

Name:	Kruger National Park
Location:	North East South Africa
Established:	1898
Area:	19,632 square km
Visitors per year:	500,000

Zebras roam in herds on the plains of Kruger National Park.

The Landscape

Kruger National Park is mainly flat with some low hills. It is a **savannah** region, which has grassy plains with a few trees, dense bush and shrubs. In the dry season there is very little rain so few plants grow. In the wet season there is some rain for the shrubs and trees. Some **subtropical** forest grows along the banks of the park's rivers.

Plant Life

In Kruger National Park the plants have developed ways to protect themselves. Many shrubs and trees have long thorns to protect them against grazing animals. The baobab tree (above) stores moisture in its large trunk for times of drought.

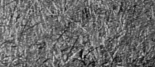

Wildlife

Kruger National Park has many different animals. There are about 250 **endangered** black rhinoceroses in the park. On the plains, giraffes, elephants, impala, zebras and buffaloes graze. Lions, tigers and leopards also search for food.

In the trees, baboons and other monkeys swing from branch to branch. Many birds including the hornbill live there, too. In the rivers, crocodiles, warthogs and hippopotamuses wallow in the water.

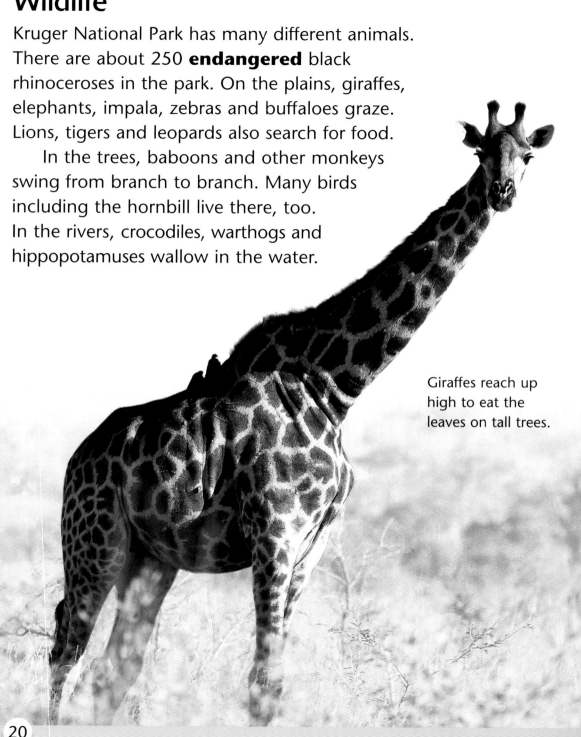

Giraffes reach up high to eat the leaves on tall trees.

People and the Park

Park rangers make sure that any park visitors don't disturb the animals. Visitors only travel around the park between sunrise and sunset. Then they spend the night in a fenced-in camp. This protects both the people and the animals.

Park rangers carry out important **conservation** work on the land, too. They make sure it is suitable for the animals. Thanks to their hard work, the animals thrive in the park.

Visitors stay in special fenced-in camps.

A group of tourists watch wildlife from a safe distance.

Uluru-Kata Tjuta National Park, Australia

Uluru-Kata Tjuta (oo-lah-ROO KAH-tah JOO-tah) National Park has the world's largest rock. It is called Uluru and is 335 metres long. It is also one of the world's oldest rocks. The park is found in central Australia. It spans over 1,200 square kilometres and has about 650 thousand visitors each year.

This area was set up as a national park in 1958 to protect the Aboriginal people and the landscape.

Name: Uluru-Kata Tjuta National Park

Location: Northern Territory, Australia

Established: 1958

Area: 1,256 square km

Visitors per year: 650,000

Uluru is an Aboriginal name meaning "great pebble".

At sunset, the domes of Kata Tjuta glow many colours. They change from pink and orange to red and purple.

The Landscape

Millions of years ago the park was an island in a lake. Then the water dried up and the land became visible. Today it is mainly flat and very dry.

In the park there is a group of large sandstone rocks called Kata Tjuta. This is a collection of thirty rocks that are found around the park. Along with Uluru, these rocks help to break up the flat landscape.

Uluru-Kata Tjuta History

This area has been sacred to the Aboriginal people of Australia for thousands of years. They called it Uluru-Kata Tjuta. When it became a national park in 1958 it was called Ayers Rock. Then in 1985 it was handed back to the Aboriginal people. They changed its name back to Uluru-Kata Tjuta.

thorny devil lizard

Wildlife

Uluru-Kata Tjuta National Park has many different animals. These animals have to survive very hot and dry conditions.

Along the plains, dingoes, red kangaroos, wallabies and possums search for food and water. Lizards, snakes and frogs crawl across the dry sand, too.

In the sky, parrots, wrens, thornbills and peregrine falcons soar and glide. In the few rock pools, shrimps dart around.

At the base of Uluru there is a waterfall.

Wallabies survive the hot climate by resting under trees.

People and the Park

Uluru-Kata Tjuta is a sacred place to the Aboriginal people so visitors are asked not to climb the rocks. Instead they hike or drive around the park. Some even ride camels.

Park rangers protect the area from **erosion** and pollution. Some park rangers are Aboriginal. They show visitors the sacred caves beneath Uluru. Inside there are paintings that describe the history and traditions of the Aboriginal people.

Aboriginal art

Camels take people around the park.

Khao Yai National Park, Thailand

Khao Yai National Park has an amazing variety of living creatures. It is found in north east Thailand. The park spans over 1 thousand square kilometres and has more than a million visitors each year.

This area was set up as Thailand's first national park in 1962. It was set up to protect the wildlife and the landscape. Today it has one of the few **rainforests** left in Thailand.

ASIA

Thailand

Name: Khao Yai National Park

Location: North East Thailand

Established: 1962

Area: 1,234 square km

Visitors per year: 1.4 million

Visitors to Khao Yai can enjoy hiking or bird-watching in the park's forests.

The Landscape

In Khao Yai National Park there are mountains, rivers, waterfalls, grasslands and rainforests. Some of the mountains are more than 1,000 metres tall.

The grasslands contain many species, but perhaps the most interesting part of the park is the **tropical** rainforest. Most of Thailand's rainforests have been destroyed for wood and farmland. However, rainforests like these are important because they support a great many of the plant and animal species on Earth.

Haeo Suwat (HAY-oh soo-waht) Waterfall is one of many waterfalls found in the park.

Layers of a Rainforest

Most plants and animals live in the canopy layer because it gets the most sun and rain. The forest floor is home to large animals that hunt on the ground, and plants that grow in damp areas, such as ferns.

emergent layer - - - - - - - - -

canopy - - - -

understorey - - - - - - -

forest floor - - - - - - - - -

Wildlife

Khao National Park has many different animals. In the **rainforest**, tigers, leopards and bears stalk among the undergrowth. In the trees, monkeys, tree frogs and gibbons travel from branch to branch. Hornbills, woodpeckers, parrots and Siamese fireback pheasants live in the trees, too.

Butterflies, bats and rare insects fill the air. Dangerous snakes slither along the ground.

Saturn butterflies are protected in the park.

There are only around 500 tigers left in Thailand.

White-handed gibbons live in the tropical rainforest.

People and the Park

Park rangers protect the animals and the rainforest. They take visitors on walks or rides through the park and to special viewing towers to look at the animals. This way the visitors can see them without disturbing them.

Sometimes visitors are allowed to stay overnight in small houses within the park.

Visitors take an elephant ride with their guide through the park's forests.

The Future of National Parks

As the world's population grows, more and more land is being used for housing. National parks are very important as they help in the **conservation** of many natural landscapes. They also save the lives of hundreds of **endangered species**.

Without national parks, many of these great wonders would not be around for us to enjoy.

This signpost tells park visitors how to behave.

Grand Canyon National Park

Glossary

alpine tundra an area that is too cold for trees to grow

canyons long, deep, narrow gorges with steep sides formed by a river

conservation the protection and management of an area and its resources

culture the customs, beliefs and values of a group of people

endangered in danger of dying out

erosion wearing away of the Earth's surface

geysers springs that shoot boiling water and steam out of the ground

glaciers slow-moving rivers of ice

habitats areas where animals or plants live

native people people descended from the population that originally lived in the area

park ranger a person who takes care of the park

plateau a large, flat raised piece of land

rainforest forests that occur in areas of heavy rainfall

savannah flat, grassy land with few trees

species a group of animals or plants that share the same characteristics and can breed together

subtropical a warm climate with limited seasonal rainfall

temperate a mild climate with distinct winter and summer seasons

terrain the shape of the land

tropical hot and humid climate

Index